# Clifford THE BIG RED DOG®

# THE RUNAWAY RABBIT

Adapted by Teddy Margulies
Drawings by Carolyn Bracken
Color by Sandrina Kurtz

## Based on the Scholastic book series
## "Clifford The Big Red Dog"
## by Norman Bridwell

From the television script
"A Bunny in a Haystack"
by Anne-Marie Perrotta and Tean Schultz

Cartwheel
·B·O·O·K·S·®

SCHOLASTIC INC.

New York   Toronto   London   Auckland   Sydney   Mexico City
New Delhi   Hong Kong

No part of this publication may be reproduced, or stored in a retrieval system, or transmitted in any form or by any means, electronic, mechanical, photocopying, recording, or otherwise, without written permission of the publisher. For information regarding permission, write to Scholastic Inc., Attention: Permissions Department, 555 Broadway, New York, NY 10012.

ISBN 0-439-21361-4

Library of Congress Cataloging-in-Publication Data available

12  13  14  15  16          04  03  02

Printed in the U.S.A.   24
First printing, February 2001

"Wally, this is Clifford,"

Emily Elizabeth said.

"Clifford, this is Wally.

Wally is our classroom

bunny," Emily Elizabeth explained.

"It's my turn to take care

of him this weekend."

"But I have to go out now,"

Emily Elizabeth said.

"Will you stay home and watch Wally?"

Clifford wagged his

tail and woofed.

"Thanks," Emily Elizabeth said.

And she waved good-bye.

Cleo and T-Bone
came to visit.
Clifford introduced
them to Wally.

"He is so cute,"
Cleo said. "Can we
take him out
and play with him?"

"Why not?" Clifford said.

"How much trouble can

a little bunny be?"

He opened the cage.

Wally wrinkled his nose.

He wiggled his ears.

Hippity-hop!

Off he went.

Wally hopped off the table.

He hopped across the floor.

Hippity-hop!

And off he went.

Clifford and his friends

dashed after him.

Wally hopped across

the yard and into

a hollow log.

T-Bone followed him.

Wally hopped out
the other end.
But T-Bone got stuck
inside the log.

There was only one
thing to do.
Clifford took a
deep breath and...

WHOOSH!

Out popped T-Bone.

But where was Wally?

The three dogs ran

here and there.

They looked high and low.

"There he is,"

Clifford said.

"There he *was!*"

Cleo said. "Gosh,

he's fast!"

Clifford, Cleo, and

T-Bone ran as fast

as they could.

But Wally was faster.

"Where did he go?"

T-Bone asked.

"I don't know,"

Clifford said.

"But I know where I
would go if *I* were
a rabbit," he added.

Clifford, Cleo, and

T-Bone raced to

Farmer Green's.

And there was Wally.

"He'll never want to
leave here," Cleo said.
"And I'm too tired to
catch and carry him."

"We may not be able
to catch Wally,"
Clifford said.
"But we *can* catch
a carrot."

Wally followed Clifford

all the way home.

Clifford led Wally

back to his cage.

Then he gave him

the carrot.

"I never thought a
little bunny could be
so much trouble,"
Cleo said.

Just then Emily Elizabeth
came home.
"Thanks for watching
Wally," she said.

"Poor Wally has been
cooped up in his cage
all day. I think I'll let him out."

Emily Elizabeth opened the door.

"Why don't you guys play

with him while I clean

his cage!" she said.

"After all, how much trouble can a little bunny be?"

# Do You Remember?

**Circle the right answer.**

1. Wally belonged to...

    a. Emily Elizabeth's best friend.

    b. Grandma.

    c. Emily Elizabeth's class.

2. Clifford, Cleo, and T-Bone found Wally...

    a. at the movie theater.

    b. at Farmer Green's.

    c. at Farmer Brown's.

**Which happened first?**
**Which happened next?**
**Which happened last?**
**Write a 1, 2, or 3 in the space**
**after each sentence.**

Clifford led Wally home with a carrot. _____

Wally ran away. _____

Emily Elizabeth asked Clifford
to watch Wally. _____

**Answers:**